A GOOFY MOVIE

Adapted by Francine Hughes

D0962378

SCHOLASTIC INC.
New York Toronto London Auckland Sydney

ISBN 0-590-22276-7

12 11 10 9 8 7 6 5 4   5 6 7 8 9/9 0/0

Printed in the U.S.A.   40

First Scholastic printing, May 1995

1

White, puffy clouds dotted the sky. A golden field stretched into the distance. Max sighed. It was the perfect setting for romance. Suddenly, he spied Roxanne.

Roxanne, his dream girl. Roxanne, the love of his life.

"Max!" Roxanne cried. "At last! You're here!"

She held out her arms.

Wow, thought Max. This is a dream come true.

He leaned forward for a kiss. But Roxanne gasped. She pulled away.

"What's wrong?" asked Max. But he already knew. He sounded different. Funny. And his front teeth were getting bigger. They hung down past his lower lip. His ears drooped down, too. And his nose! It was growing . . . growing . . . growing.

Roxanne took one more horrified look at him. Then she ran.

"Ahyuck!" said Max. He sounded ridiculous. He looked ridiculous. In fact, he sounded and looked just like his dad.

This wasn't a dream come true. It was a nightmare. Max had turned into his father!

"Ahhh!" he screamed.

Max woke up with a start. He checked his teeth, his ears, and his nose. Everything was normal.

"Whew," he said. "It *was* all a dream."

Max snuggled back into bed and tried to fall asleep. He wanted to get back to the good part of the dream. The part where

Roxanne held out her arms. Ah. There she was. Pretty as a picture.

B-r-i-n-g! Groggily, Max reached for the phone.

"Hello?"

"Where are you?" cried his best friend, P.J. "You should have been here an hour ago."

"What?" Max grabbed the clock. He had overslept! Overslept on the most important day of the year! No. The most important day of his life. It was the last day of school, and he was going to be late!

Max leaped out of bed.

"Maybe we should call the whole thing off," P.J. continued on the phone.

"No way!" Max whirled around, looking for his pants. The phone cord was wrapped around him like a mummy. There! His pants were on the chair. Still wrapped in the cord, Max stepped into his jeans.

"It's the last day of junior high," he told P.J. "I've been trying to get Roxanne to notice me all year. This is it. The time for our plan. It's now or never."

"Well, you better get a move on," said P.J. "I'll meet you at school." *Click!!* He hung up.

Max tried to hang up, too. He spun around, unwinding the phone cord. *Whoosh!* His pants dropped to the floor. Max bent over to pull them back up.

Just then Goofy barged into the room. "Morning, son!" he said cheerfully.

Quickly, Max tugged up his pants. He clutched them around his waist and shot Goofy an angry look. "Dad!"

"Oops!" said Goofy. He backed out of the room. "Sorry. I forgot you like your privacy now."

Goofy quietly closed the door behind him. A second later, he knocked. Then, without waiting for an answer, he barreled in once again.

"Morning, son," he said just as cheerfully as before. "Do you have any clothes that need washing?"

Max waved his arm around the room. "Help yourself," he said.

Piles of clothes covered his bed, his desk, and all the furniture. Only one corner was mess-free. In that corner stood a cardboard cutout. It was a rock 'n' roll star playing the guitar.

Goofy crossed his arms. He tried to be stern. "Max, we talked about the mess. . . ."

Max was busy getting dressed. "I'll take care of it later," he said. Hurriedly, he tied his sneakers and raced for the door.

"Oof!" He ran right into Goofy.

"What's the big rush?" asked Goofy. He held Max firmly in place. "I'll drive you to school on my way to work."

Max stopped struggling. He stood stock still, fear in his eyes. His dad drive him to school? Where other kids would see them? Together?

"Uh . . . no, thanks, Dad. I'll walk. I need the exercise."

Once again Goofy eyed the messy bedroom. Then he pulled in the vacuum cleaner. *Pffft!* One by one, Max's dirty clothes disappeared up the nozzle.

Thunk! The cardboard cutout got sucked up, too.

"Dad!" cried Max. He tried to tug the cardboard back out. Finally, he switched off the vacuum.

The cutout popped free. But its head looked like an accordion.

"You ruined it, Dad."

"Sorry," said Goofy. "Who was he, anyway?"

Max shook his head. Didn't his dad know anything? "Only Powerline," he said. "The biggest rock star on the planet."

The next instant Max was out the door. He had to hurry. He had to get to school.

Goofy ran out behind him. "Wait!" he told Max. "You forgot something." He handed Max his lunchbox. Then he kissed him good-bye.

A bunch of kids, standing close by, snickered. Max turned red. Why did his father always embarrass him? Hunching his shoulders, he walked off towards school.

Everyone laughs at me, he thought. But that's going to change.

I have a plan!

2

At school, Max stood on top of the football field bleachers. He squared his shoulders, ready for anything.

Except the stairs.

Crash! Boom! Bang! Max tumbled down the bleacher steps.

All around him, Max heard kids laughing. He shut his eyes to block out the noise.

Bang! Boom! Crash! Max hit the ground. Hard.

"Are you all right?" a soft voice asked.

Max opened one eye. Roxanne knelt by his side.

"Hi," she said sweetly.

Max smiled. He opened his mouth to say "hi" back. But he was too nervous. He could only laugh. "Ahyuck!"

Ahyuck? That's all he could say?

Max had to get away. He had to escape. Jumping up, he crashed into a garbage can. The noise echoed up and down the field.

What did Roxanne think of him now? But Max didn't dare look at her again. Instead, he hurried into school.

Inside the building, everybody chattered about the last day of school.

Max stomped down the hall. "Roxanne says hi," he said to himself. "And I say, 'ahyuck.' I can't believe it!"

He leaned against his locker, disgusted.

P.J. ran over. "Where have you been?" he asked, out of breath. P.J. wasn't in very good shape. And he'd been running all around, trying to find Max. "I have the camera."

P.J. opened his jacket. He showed Max the camcorder hidden inside. "My dad will kill me if he finds out I have this. Are you sure you want to do it? Go through with the plan?"

Max nodded. "To Roxanne, I'm just a nobody. But after today — "

Max stopped short, blinded by a bright light. The light glared from a cart filled with electronic equipment. There was a slide projector, a sound system, CD player, and tons and tons of wires.

Max rubbed his hands together. "Hey, Bobby!" he said to the boy pushing the cart. "This is all for us? It's going to be great!"

Bobby pushed his glasses up on his nose. "I need funds," he said, holding out his hand.

"Oh, that's right," said Max. "Your fee." He handed Bobby a spray can filled with cheese spread. *Spritz!* Bobby shot a stream of cheese into his mouth.

"Mmm." He grinned. "Let's do it!"

* * *

The junior high auditorium was packed for the last assembly. Excited, kids yelled and laughed and jumped out of their seats.

Onstage, the class president shouted to be heard.

"Yea to all of us for, like, a really neat year," Stacey said. "And you are all invited to my end-of-school party next Saturday. We can watch the Powerline concert on TV."

Principal Mazur spoke next. "Thank you, Stacey," he said in his dull, boring voice. "And good morning, boys and girls. You know, boys and girls, every year . . ."

Bit by bit, the room quieted. Everybody had fallen asleep. Students snored softly. But the principal didn't notice. He just went on and on. Behind Principal Mazur, a giant screen came down onstage. A few kids opened their eyes. This wasn't on the program. Something was up.

Suddenly the lights went out. And Principal Mazur dropped through a trapdoor. "What's going oooooon?" he shouted.

Then everyone woke up. A picture of Powerline filled the screen. Only it wasn't really Powerline. It was Max, wearing a Powerline costume and sunglasses!

Bobby had set up all the equipment. Now P.J. was filming Max backstage, so Max appeared on-screen at the very same time.

Their plan had gone into action!

A Powerline song blasted from the speakers. Max pretended to sing. He mouthed the words to the song as the music played.

Max whirled around in a Powerline move. But his foot got caught in a wire.

"Whoah!" he cried, falling . . . falling . . . falling . . . right through the screen.

Rip!

Max rolled onstage. The crowd jumped to its feet with a roar. Max couldn't believe it. They were cheering for *him*!

Roxanne stood in the front row. Max spun around, ready to carry out his plan.

He sang to Roxanne. They were nose to

nose. Max leaned in close, then leaped away, striking a pose.

The crowd buzzed. Who was that guy?

P.J. crawled up to Max. He tied a rope to Max's belt. The rope hung down from the ceiling, like a pulley. Bobby tugged the other end. *Whoosh!* Max soared off the ground, over everyone's head, while he sang out to the crowd.

Slowly, Bobby lowered Max. Now he dangled above Roxanne.

This is it, Max thought. My big moment.

All at once, the music stopped. The rope went slack, and Max tumbled to the ground — right by Principal Mazur's feet!

Uh-oh, Max thought.

"I'm back," the principal said. "And I'm going to find out who you are." He pulled off Max's sunglasses.

The audience gasped. "It's the Goof boy!" one boy shouted.

3

Max sat in the principal's office. Upset with everything, he waited to meet his fate.

"I'm a failure," he moaned. "I'm in trouble with the principal. And I blew it with Roxanne. She still thinks I'm a dweeb."

Max buried his face in his hands. He didn't see Roxanne and Stacey whispering at the door.

Stacey pushed Roxanne inside. "Talk to him!" she hissed.

"Ahem," said Roxanne shyly.

Max moaned again, not hearing.

Roxanne shifted her books. "Ahem!" she said a little louder.

Max didn't lift his head.

"Tap him!" Stacey ordered.

Roxanne tapped his shoulder. Surprised, Max jumped up. *Thud!* He knocked Roxanne's books to the floor.

Max was so surprised, he couldn't talk. Finally he sputtered, "G-g-gosh! I'm sorry."

Roxanne knelt to gather her books. "It's okay. Really."

Max bent down to help. His hand brushed hers. Their eyes locked. Then Max looked away, embarrassed. What would she think of him now?

"I . . . I liked your Powerline dance," Roxanne said softly.

It took a minute. But then it sunk in. Roxanne liked his dance!

"It's from Powerline's new video," Max told her eagerly. "He's doing a concert next week in Los Angeles."

"I know!" said Roxanne. "Stacey's having a party so everybody can watch it on TV."

Max took a deep breath. It's now or never, he thought.

"Um, Roxanne. I was sort of kind of thinking . . . can you go . . . with me? To the party, I mean."

Roxanne ducked her head. "Well, I was sort of kind of thinking . . . I'd love to."

"Yeah?" said Max, surprised.

"Yeah," said Stacey, pulling Roxanne away.

Max grinned. Then he did a little dance of joy. In mid-step, Principal Mazur opened his office door. He pointed at Max. Max froze.

"Get that boy's father on the phone," he barked to his secretary. "At once!"

4

Goofy was at The Children's Portrait Studio, working. "Smiley-wiley-iley," he gurgled to a baby girl. "Please!" He wanted to take her picture.

The baby gave a small smile.

"Step aside, Goofy." Goofy's co-worker Pete pushed him away. "Let a pro show you how it's done."

Pete made a grab for the baby.

"Waah!" she screamed, crawling off.

"Kids love me." Pete chased after the

baby. "Why, my son, P.J., is begging me to take him on vacation this summer."

Goofy thought about Max. He wouldn't want to go on vacation with *his* dad. Not now. Probably not ever.

"We're going camping," Pete continued. "The great outdoors brings father and son close together."

"Really?" said Goofy. He scooped up the baby and gave her a stuffed toy. Immediately, she stopped crying. "Max would never go for anything like that."

Pete huffed and puffed, tired from his baby chase. "Something's wrong when a son won't go camping with his dad. Maybe Max is up to no good. Maybe he's in trouble in school. Watch out! He could wind up in jail."

"Nah," said Goofy. "Max is a good — "

"Goofy, line seven," a voice said over the store loudspeaker. "Goofy, line seven."

Goofy picked up the telephone.

"Mr. Goof," said Principal Mazur. "Your son's up to no good."

What? thought Goofy.

"He's in trouble at school," the principal went on. "Watch out. Or he'll wind up in jail."

A minute later, Goofy hung up the phone. Max in trouble? Max in jail? Goofy slumped against the wall. What am I going to do? he wondered.

A sudden thought popped into his head. Camping! The great outdoors! He remembered camping with his own dad. The fun they had. The experiences they shared.

Lake Destiny, Idaho, was the place. Goofy snapped his fingers. He and Max were going fishing!

5

Max sauntered home from school. Chants of "Max! Max! Max!" still rang in his ears. Everybody cheered for him. Football players. Popular kids. Everybody!

At last, Max thought. Everything's perfect.

Outside his house, he stopped short. Goofy was loading the car with camping gear.

"There!" Goofy said. He tossed a patched-up tent on top of the roof rack.

"Going somewhere?" asked Max.

Goofy plopped a fishing hat on his head. "Sure are, pal-a-roony."

"Cool," said Max. "Have a good time."

"But, Max. This isn't just my vacation. It's a vacation with my best buddy."

"Donald Duck?" said Max.

Goofy flung his arm around his son. "No, silly. With you."

Then Goofy jammed a fishing hat on Max's head, too. Goofy sniffed, tears in his eyes. "You look like me when I was your age."

Max stepped back. This was worse than his nightmare!

"Wait!" said Goofy. "I saved the best for last."

He reached into a box and pulled out an old wooden fishing pole.

"You saved a stick?" Max said.

"No, silly." Goofy's chest swelled with pride. "This is a fishing pole. It's been handed down from Goof to Goof to Goof. And now it's yours, son. To use on our fishing trip."

Max blinked. "Fishing trip?"

"Yup. Just like my dad and I took. We're going to the same place. Lake Destiny." Goofy unfolded a dusty yellow map. "We're even using the same map."

Max peered at the map. A red line ran from their home all the way to Lake Destiny, Idaho. "That trip will take weeks, Dad. And there's this party . . ."

"There will be lots of time for parties later," Goofy interrupted. "When I was your age, I was never invited to parties. Now look at me!"

Max looked at Goofy. In his bulky fishing vest and fishing hat, he seemed sillier than ever.

Goofy opened the car door. "Hop in, Maxie."

"No."

"Aw, come on. Hop in."

Max dug in his heels. "No, Dad."

"Right in there."

"No."

Goofy finally pushed him inside. "I don't

want you in jail," he said. "I'm not giving up on you. We'll work it out. Together."

"What are you talking about?" Max asked, confused.

But already, Goofy was driving away.

"Good-bye, house! Good-bye, mailbox!" Goofy backed over their picket fence. "Good-bye, broken pile of wood!"

Max slumped in his seat. Good-bye, hopes, he thought. Good-bye, dreams. Good-bye, Roxanne.

6

At least Goofy agreed to stop by Roxanne's house before their trip. Max had to talk to her. He had to tell her what had happened.

"I'm really looking forward to the party," Roxanne told Max. They were sitting on her front porch.

"I was, too," Max said sadly.

Roxanne sat up straight. *"Was?"*

You see," Max explained, "my dad wants to go on this trip."

"Don't worry. I understand," Roxanne

said. "I'm sure I can find someone else to go with."

Max jumped to his feet. "Someone else?"

Roxanne nodded. She stood up, then edged towards the front door. "Well, I'll see you later."

Max had to act — and quickly. He couldn't lose her. Not now! He hopped from one foot to the other. What could he say? What could he do?

He had it!

"But, Roxanne," he said, "I *have* to take this family vacation. We're going to Los Angeles. My dad's taking me to the Powerline concert."

Roxanne stopped in her tracks. "Powerline?"

Max went on, hurriedly. "My dad . . . uh . . . knows Powerline!"

Roxanne smiled, walking back to Max. "Really?"

"Really. So please don't go to the party with anyone else. I want to wave to you when we join Powerline onstage."

Roxanne moved closer. "Onstage? This is incredible!"

Max ducked his head. "I wouldn't miss our date for just anything. It had to be an incredible something!"

Roxanne moved closer still. Then she kissed Max on the cheek.

Surprised and pleased, Max stumbled down the porch steps and into the car.

Suddenly everything seemed wonderful. The world was bathed in rosy colors. Max sniffed the air. Flowers! He smelled lovely flowers. He could even hear violins playing. Roxanne had kissed him! Nothing could go wrong!

Goofy drove away with a jerk. Max was flung against his seat. And just like that, the real world crashed back.

Max snapped to attention. Why did he make up that stupid Powerline story? And those crazy promises! He could never keep them. Why had he lied?

Max closed his eyes. I'm in deep sludge, he thought.

*　　*　　*

While Max thought about Roxanne, Goofy drove through the countryside. One hand gripped the wheel. His other hand held the camcorder.

Goofy turned to film Max. "How about a wave?"

Screech! They swerved all over the road.

"Not now!" shouted Max. Quickly he covered the lens.

Goofy grinned. "Ahyuck! You are such a kidder. How about playing a game?"

Max didn't want to. He didn't want to sing songs. And he didn't want to talk, either. He was too upset about Roxanne.

Goofy spread the map over the steering wheel. They swerved again.

Max gulped. This could get dangerous.

"Hey!" he said. "Why don't I hold the map?"

Goofy shook his head. "I don't know. Finding our way is a big responsibility. You might not be ready for it. Besides, I have a surprise for you right up the road."

Goofy pressed the gas pedal. They zoomed around the curve on two wheels. Then Goofy braked to a halt. *Screech!* They were in front of an old faded sign. Lester's Possum Park.

"First stop!" Goofy crowed.

7

Goofy drove through the entrance to Lester's Park. It was a giant opossum mouth opened wide.

Inside the park, Max gazed around. He saw overgrown grass. Skinny bare trees. Little kids screaming.

Ugh, he thought.

"It's even better than I remember!" said Goofy. "Come on!"

Goofy pulled Max out of the car. He dragged him close to an old rotting stage.

"Howdy, folks," an actor was saying. He

wore overalls and a straw hat and chewed an old pipe. "You're just in time for the Possum Jamboree!"

The ratty curtain parted. The audience gasped as the opossum puppet, made from old tin cans and wooden crates, waved its arm.

There was a loud click. Then a recording came on. Creaking, the opossum moved its mouth.

"Who's your favorite opossum?" the puppet asked.

"Lester!" shouted the crowd. "Lester!"

Three other opossums popped up. "Now gather round my opossum pals," said Lester, "and join the jamboree."

Goofy's grin got even wider. "Let's sit up front," he whispered to Max.

Reluctantly, Max sat down in the first row. All around him, babies and toddlers hooted and hollered with the opossums. Max was the only teenager.

"It's yodeling time!" cried Lester.

Goofy jumped up. "Yo-de-lay-he-ho!" He yodeled louder and longer than anyone else.

Max made himself as small as he could. He wanted to disappear.

After the show, Goofy spotted a souvenir stand. Off he went. Alone at last, Max leaned against a tree. Would they ever leave this place?

"I could stay here all week!" cried Goofy, coming back with a souvenir for Max. He plopped a furry cap on Max's head. It was opossum-shaped — and it smelled like the animal, too!

Goofy pushed him toward a tree. Two opossums hung by their tails on a branch. A photographer stood nearby.

"What say we get our picture taken with the opossums?" said Goofy, skipping away.

Max tried to ignore him. But Goofy wouldn't give up.

"Hey, son! I'm over here!" He climbed the tree and hung upside down — right next to the animals. "We're almost ready for the picture," he called to the photographer. "Come on, Maxie!"

Max edged a bit closer.

Then a seven-year-old boy laughed. "Hey, everybody!" he shouted. "Check out the dork in the tree!"

Max stopped moving.

"Say 'sassafras,' " the photographer told Goofy.

"Sassyfras!" cried Goofy.

Suddenly the branch snapped. Goofy hit the ground with a thud. The opossums flew through the air. *Smack!* They hit Max full in the face. Trying to run away, the animals scurried down his shirt.

"Whoah!" shouted Max, jumping all around.

Goofy thought Max was finally having fun. "That's the spirit, son," he said. He jumped around, too.

Max pulled the opossums out of his shirt. But Goofy kept dancing. He reached for Max.

"No, Dad!" cried Max.

Goofy lifted him off the ground. Then he spun him around and around.

"Stop!" Max begged. "Ple-e-e-ease!"

At last Goofy ended the dance. He twirled Max one final time. Then he pulled him onto his knee for the big finish. "Ta-dah!"

The seven-year-old snorted. "Hey! It's Dork and Dork Junior!"

Feeling worse than ever, Max threw off his opossum cap. He stomped away, leaving Goofy all alone.

8

Goofy caught up to Max in the Possum parking lot. "Max! Where are you going?"

"I'm trying to get away from you!" said Max. His face was still bright red.

"Me! What did I do?" Goofy asked. "I thought we were having fun."

Max didn't answer. Instead he got in the car and slammed the door. "Let's just go!" he shouted.

Goofy got in beside him. "You dropped your hat," he said. He handed Max the opossum cap.

In a flash, Max threw it out the window. *Splat!* The cap landed in a mud puddle.

"Grrr," Max growled. "This is the stupidest vacation. You drag me away from home. You jam me in this dumb car. Then you drive a million miles to see a bunch of rats!"

Max closed his eyes. "Wake me when the trip's over."

Goofy shook his head, stunned. Slowly, he drove away from Possum Park. What was going on? He'd never seen Max act like this!

Lightning flashed. The sky grew dark. Then the rain came flooding down.

Perfect, thought Max. The perfect end to a perfect morning.

A few hours later, Max and Goofy came to a campground. Goofy parked the car at the edge of a lake. The skies had cleared. The sun was setting. Goofy sighed. It was all so beautiful. If only Max could enjoy it with him.

"You want to get some fishing practice in?" Goofy asked hopefully. "We'll be getting to Lake Destiny in just a few days now. You can try out the Goof fishing pole."

Max turned his back on Goofy. "Maybe later."

Feeling defeated, Goofy set up their tent. Who am I kidding? he thought. This trip isn't working at all.

Suddenly, the ground began to shake. A huge truck rumbled over. It passed right over Goofy's tent, two wheels on either side. Goofy squinted in the cave-like darkness. The truck had blocked the sun.

Goofy stepped out from underneath. The truck was really a camper. And it unfolded right before his eyes. First, basketball courts sprang up. Then a giant pool appeared. On the roof, a bowling alley popped out. Goofy couldn't see the sun, the trees, or the lake. The camper had turned into a grand hotel.

"Wow! Now that's camping!" Max said, running up.

"You can say that again," said the driver. He opened his cab door, hitting Goofy on the head.

The voice sounded familiar. Goofy shook his head to clear it. "Pete?" he said.

Inside the camper, P.J. was dancing to a Powerline tape. "Max!" he said when he saw his friend. "Small wilderness! Would you like to borrow some of my Powerline moves?"

Max grinned. "You can keep the moves. But I wouldn't mind having this camper. You're a lucky man, P.J."

"Me?" P.J. looked surprised. "You're the star. And you'll be onstage with Powerline. It's unbelievable."

Max gulped. His lie! How did P.J. know about it? "Who told you that?"

"Everybody in town knows about it, Max. You're going to be famous." P.J. paused a moment, then added, "especially with Roxanne."

Max's heart dropped. Roxanne . . . the kids in school . . . everybody in town . . .

they all thought he'd be appearing on TV with Powerline. Only one person didn't know about it. His dad.

On the roof of the camper, Pete stood in front of a bowling lane. "So, Goofy, how are things with Max?"

Goofy shrugged. "Everything I try drives us further apart. Maybe I should just back off."

"Wrong, Goof." Pete cracked his knuckles, getting ready to bowl. "You've got to keep kids under your thumb."

Goofy checked his thumb. There was nothing there. Then he understood what Pete meant. You have to watch kids every step of the way. You have to be tough.

Pete picked up a ball and hurled it down the lane. Nine pins fell. One was left.

"Watch this," Pete told Goofy. "This is how to do it."

"P.J.!" he called.

An instant later, P.J. stood by his

side. Max followed behind, much more slowly.

"Here, sir!" said P.J.

Pete glanced at Goofy. "Watch and learn," he mouthed. Then he pointed down the alley. Immediately, P.J. ran to the standing pin and kicked it down.

"Strike!" shouted Pete, laughing. "Say, Goof, why don't you stay for dinner?"

"Cool!" said Max.

At the very same moment, Goofy said, "No, thanks. Max and I have some fish to catch."

"Aw, Dad. We can do that tomorrow."

Goofy looked down. "Well . . ." he said weakly.

Pete cleared his throat. He held up his thumb and looked at Goofy.

"Remember," Goofy told himself. "Under your thumb." Out loud, he said, "Maximilian!" He tried to sound stern. "Get your gear. We're going fishing."

Max didn't move.

"Now!" said Goofy.

Max jumped. In a huff, he marched away. Pete turned his thumb the other way. He gave Goofy the thumb's up sign.

Proud of himself, Goofy strode after Max.

9

Sunlight sparkled like diamonds on the lake. Birds chirped, and then fell still. It was a lovely, peaceful afternoon.

"But Dad!" Max shrieked. "I don't know how to fish!"

Goofy plopped the fishing hat on Max's head. "Come on, Max. That never stopped me. I'll show you a family secret handed down through 13 Goof generations. The Perfect Cast."

"The Perfect what?" said Max.

"Cast. You know. When you let go of the

fishing line and let it fly. Now, stand with your feet apart."

Goofy stood with his legs spread wide. A little too wide — he almost fell down.

"Oops!" he said, getting his balance.

"Now you start with the rod at ten o'clock." Goofy lifted his arm, and brought the fishing rod over his shoulder. Then he swung it forward. The rod stopped a little over his head — where the ten would be if Goofy was standing in the center of a clock.

"Two o'clock."

Goofy brought it forward a bit.

"*Tour jeté.*"

He did a ballerina jump.

"Twist."

He twisted right and left.

"I'm a little teapot."

Goofy held out the fishing pole like a teapot spout and pretended to pour.

"The windup."

Goofy wound up like a baseball pitcher. *Whizzzz!* The fishing line spun out behind him. It sailed through the air. Over the camp. And it hooked a big juicy steak on Pete's grill.

"Now we let her fly," said Goofy. He gave a big tug on the line.

The steak flew up, up, up, then down, down, down. *Splat!* It landed in a giant footprint. Next to the giant footprint was the giant himself. The big hairy creature called Bigfoot!

Bigfoot sniffed at the steak. He licked his lips.

"Finally we reel her in," said Goofy.

Bigfoot's mouth watered. He opened wide — just as Goofy yanked the line.

The steak flew out of Bigfoot's reach. *Splash!* It hit the lake. Bigfoot chased after it. He dove into the water. A second later he came up. The steak was in his mouth.

But Goofy just thought he had a catch.

"Quick! Get the camera," he called to Max. "I've got a big one."

Max ran for the camera. And Goofy

pulled in the line with all his strength. "Must be over 300 pounds," he said, panting.

Bigfoot churned through the water.

Max handed the camera to Goofy. With one hand, Goofy worked the camcorder. With the other hand, he reeled in Bigfoot.

"Uh, D-d-d-dad," Max stammered. "It's Bigfoot."

"Oh," said Goofy. "Would you back up a bit, Mr. Foot?" he asked, politely. "You're out of focus."

"ROAR!"

Bigfoot let go of the steak and lunged for Goofy and Max. The steak soared up in the air. It came down on Pete's head.

"What's the big idea?" Pete said.

In answer, Goofy and Max raced by. Bigfoot was hot on their heels. *Roar!*

"Bigfoot!" cried Pete. He ran for the camper. In two seconds flat, the swimming pool, the basketball court, and the bowling alley all folded back up. Pete drove off in a panic.

"Dad! Dad! What about me?" P.J. shouted, giving chase. The two disappeared down the road.

Meanwhile, Goofy and Max had almost reached their car. "Behold the Big Hairy Beast," said Goofy, still filming Bigfoot.

"Oh!" he tripped over the tent and dropped the camera. Bigfoot was closing in.

Max reached the car. He tugged at the door. "It's locked!"

"*Grrr!*" Bigfoot was almost on top of them.

Goofy left the camera right where it was. "Quick!" he cried. "The sunroof!"

Max and Goofy dove through the opening. Bigfoot leaped onto the roof right after them. Quickly, Goofy cranked it shut.

Bigfoot scratched his head, confused. Then he rocked the car back and forth.

"Whoah!" Inside, Goofy and Max tumbled all about.

Suddenly, Bigfoot stopped. He leaped off the car. He began to nose around their camping gear.

"Do you know what?" Goofy told Max. "We have Bigfoot on tape!"

"Yeah!" said Max. For the first time on the trip, he was excited. "We can sell it to TV stations and newspapers. We'll be rich!"

Max grinned happily. But his smile soon faded. Bigfoot had the camcorder.

First, he examined it carefully. Maybe it will be okay, Max thought. Maybe he'll just put it down.

Then Bigfoot pressed the eject button. The tape popped out. Bigfoot wrapped it around and around his paw — until it looked like a ball of string. The tape was ruined.

Max sighed. "Let's get out of here," he said to Goofy.

Goofy reached into his pants pocket for the car key. It wasn't there. He reached into his other pants pocket. Then he lifted his fishing hat and checked his head.

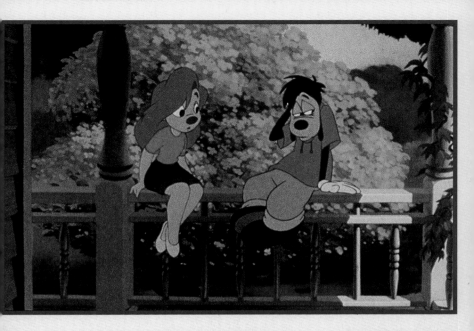

"Uh-oh," he said.

Outside, Bigfoot dangled the keys.

Max sank down in his seat. His dad had dropped the camcorder *and* the keys! Now they couldn't go anywhere. Max was trapped. Worse yet, he wasn't alone.

He was trapped with his dad.

10

Hours passed in the car. Max grew hungry. Through the windshield, he watched Bigfoot. The creature stomped all over their food. He pawed through their supplies. He tried on their clothes.

"I'm starving," Max announced.

Bigfoot kicked around a few more items. A can of soup landed on the car roof.

"Alphabet soup coming up!" Goofy said cheerfully. He cranked open the roof. Quickly, he reached up and pulled the can inside. Using the car's cigarette lighter, Goofy heated up the soup.

There was a long silence. Then Goofy giggled.

"What's so funny?" asked Max.

Goofy pointed at the can. "HI DAD Soup. Remember?"

Max shrugged.

"Sure, you remember," said Goofy. "You used to spell out sentences. Like HI DAD." He looked at Max. "Or I LOVE YOU."

Goofy stopped talking. Had he said too much? Pushed too hard? Again they sat in silence. With a start, Goofy remembered the soup. Using his two front teeth, he punched holes in the top.

"Wow! Where did you learn that?" asked Max, amazed.

Goofy smiled. "My dad taught me when we went camping."

"You two did a lot together," Max said.

Max and Goofy never did anything together. Max didn't want to. And really, all

Goofy wanted to do was hang out. Why am I so mean to him? Max wondered.

Max started to apologize. "I'm sor — "

But Goofy was talking at the same time. "Listen — "

They both fell silent. Max took a sip from the can. When he handed it to Goofy, he had a soup mustache.

Max looks just like a little boy, Goofy thought. My little boy. He felt a lump in his throat.

"What's wrong?" said Max.

"Nothing." Goofy eyed Bigfoot curled up like a baby on the roof of the car. "We might as well get some shut-eye. I don't think we can go anywhere tonight." He stretched and yawned.

"Uh, Dad." Max tapped Goofy on the shoulder. He showed him the almost empty soup can. At the bottom, he had spelled HI DAD.

"Hi, Max," Goofy whispered back. His eyes filled with tears of joy. Then he fell fast asleep.

Max listened to Goofy snore. He tried to sleep, too. But he tossed and turned. Then he tossed and turned some more. He couldn't fall asleep. So he decided to write a postcard to Roxanne.

"Dear Roxanne," he wrote. "Dad and I are having a great time. We're almost to L.A. I can hardly wait for the concert."

Here I go, thought Max. I'm lying again! It just didn't feel right. Max tore up the postcard.

"Dear Roxanne," he wrote on a new postcard. "I'm sorry I lied to you. You may never talk to me again. But I'm not going to the Powerline concert."

"Oh, man," he moaned. "I'm in trouble no matter what." Max tore that postcard up, too.

Feeling angry, he kicked the glove compartment. The door banged open. Then the map rolled out, with a red pencil right behind it. Max blinked. The map was open.

And the pencil pointed right to L.A.

Suddenly, Max had an idea. An idea that would solve his problems. Quietly, he erased the line tracing the way to Lake Destiny. In its place, he penciled in a new route. The route to L.A.

11

The next morning Bigfoot was gone. Goofy found the car keys and gathered their gear. Then they headed to a restaurant.

"I think we need to talk." Goofy stopped eating his breakfast. He turned to Max. In his hand, he held the map.

Max choked on his cereal. Did Goofy know he had changed the route?

"You should take some responsibility. I think you're ready for it now." Goofy stood, facing everyone in the restaurant. "Excuse me," he said. "Can I have your attention, please?"

Goofy tapped Max on each shoulder with the map. "I hereby name my son Official Navigator."

Everyone clapped as Goofy passed the map to Max.

"I'm not looking at the map anymore," he told Max. "You direct us. Just follow the red line. You can pick all the stops to Lake Destiny, too. I trust you, son."

Goofy lifted his orange juice in a toast. "To the open road," he said.

"To the open road," Max echoed. Goofy had made things so easy! Max was in charge of the map. In charge of where they went. Still, Max felt a little unsure. He knew he was playing a mean trick.

"It will work out," he told himself. "It has to!"

For the next few days, Max guided Goofy this way and that. Up that road, down this one. When he talked, Goofy listened. And when Goofy talked, Max listened, too. The views were beautiful. The weather, sunny.

Max began to enjoy himself.

Then, one afternoon, he led Goofy to the Neptune Inn Motel.

Fishing nets hung from the ceiling in their room. Fish swam in the waterbeds. Shells covered the furniture. And a mermaid lamp lit the room.

"Good choice, navigator," Goofy told Max.

Max swelled with pride. He liked being the navigator. He felt important. In fact, this vacation was turning out to be fun!

Just then Pete and P.J. barged into the room.

"I need some electricity for the camper," said Pete. "Can we use one tiny little outlet?"

Minutes later, giant cords snaked around the entire room. There were wires and plugs everywhere.

Looking for space, Max and P.J. went outside. There, Max told P.J. about changing the map.

"Oh, man! You are set!" said P.J.

"I don't know." Max kicked a pebble. "Things are different now. Dad and I are having a good time. This trip means a lot to him."

P.J. hopped up and down. "You have to go through with it," he said. "What about Roxanne? The kids in school?"

P.J. went on and on. Max just listened. And a little farther away, Pete listened, too. Behind a bush, he rubbed his hands. He couldn't wait to tell Goofy.

"Your son is fooling you!" Pete told Goofy excitedly. "Max changed the map. You're heading to L.A.!"

Goofy didn't believe him. "I trust my son. Maybe Max isn't perfect. But he wouldn't do that. He loves me."

"Love, shmove," said Pete. "It doesn't mean a thing. Check the map."

Slowly Goofy walked around the motel grounds. He passed by the car and stopped.

What if . . . ? he wondered. Nah. Not Max. Not my boy.

Still . . . Goofy slipped inside. Should he check the map? Shouldn't he?

No! He'd trust his son! Turning to leave, Goofy knocked into the steering wheel. *Pop!* The glove compartment opened — just the way it had for Max. Out rolled the map. Goofy snuck a look. The red line led right to L.A.

12

That night, Goofy barely spoke to Max. The next morning they got ready to leave the motel. And still, Goofy kept quiet.

Even on the road, Goofy drove silently.

Max knew something was wrong. He tried to get Goofy to sing songs. To play games. Or even just to talk. But Goofy shook his head. He was crushed. His son had lied to him!

Still, Goofy thought hopefully, there's time for Max to change his mind. The big turn is coming up. If we make a right, we hit Idaho and Lake Destiny. Make a left, and it's on to L.A. and Powerline. Maybe Max wouldn't go through with it. Maybe they'd take their fishing trip, after all.

"Here comes the turn," Goofy said, finally speaking. "Just follow my route on the map and we'll be fine."

Nervous, Max opened the map. His hands shook. Should he lead them to L.A., or not?

"Now, Max," said Goofy. "This is it. Left or right?"

"Er . . . oh . . . uh." They were coming to the divider.

"Come on, Max!"

"Eh . . ."

"Max!"

"Go . . . uh . . . left!" Max shouted.

Goofy swerved left at the last second. His heart dropped. They were on the road to L.A. Pete was right. Love didn't mean a thing. You had to be tough. Mean. Kids had to be afraid of you.

Still feeling nervous, Max glanced at

Goofy. Goofy looked upset. Gloomy. He looked . . . just like I did when we started the trip, Max thought.

This wasn't any fun. Max reached for the camcorder. He turned it on. "How about a wave?" he said to Goofy. "How about we stop for some HI DAD soup? Or even some fishing?"

Suddenly, Goofy skidded to a stop. The view was beautiful — a steep canyon with a river running through it. But Goofy didn't care. He stomped to the railing. He didn't even take the camcorder!

Max jumped out of the car. He'd never seen Goofy act like this. His dad was furious. What could be the reason? Did he know about the directions?

All of a sudden, Max didn't care about the reason. He wanted to tell Goofy the truth. He didn't want to hurt him.

"Listen, Dad," he said. "About my directions — "

Goofy walked away.

"Listen!" Max pleaded. "I've got to tell you something."

Goofy turned his back.

"Aw, gee!" Max kicked the car tire.

The car started to move. Slowly at first, so Max didn't notice. Then it gathered speed. Soon it was rolling down the canyon road!

"Dad!" shouted Max. "The car!"

"What about it?" said Goofy. His back still turned to Max, he had no interest in the car. Or anything.

"Look at it!" cried Max.

Slowly Goofy turned. He looked. Then he looked again. "THE CAR!"

13

Max and Goofy raced downhill. But they couldn't catch the car.

Suitcases and camping gear fell off the roof rack. Max and Goofy dodged the falling objects. "There's the skateboard!" Max cried.

Together, they jumped onboard. *Zoom!* Bit by bit, they gained on the car. Finally, they caught up to it.

Max grabbed hold of the door handle. He opened it. First Goofy scrambled inside. Then Max followed.

The car jounced along, out of control. "Put the brake on!" Max cried.

Goofy pulled the brake — right out of the floor. *Crash!* They broke through a guard rail.

"You ruin everything!" shouted Max.

"Me?" said Goofy as they sailed above the canyon. "You ruined the vacation."

Max and Goofy shouted at each other while the car whirled around and around. Then they dropped straight down . . . down past canyon walls . . . past goats nibbling on grass . . . down into the rushing water below. *Splash!*

"Help! Help!" Goofy and Max were thrown out of the car.

Quickly Max grabbed hold of Goofy. He pushed him up on the car roof. Then he scrambled up beside him.

"You should have let me stay home." Max continued the conversation as the car floated down the river.

"Why?" asked Goofy. "So you could wind

up in jail? Your principal called me. I know about your trouble at school."

What did jail have to do with anything? Max wondered. Out loud he said, "It's not what you think."

"You lied to me," Goofy went on.

"I had to, Dad," Max explained. "You were ruining my life."

"I only wanted to take my boy fishing."

Wham! The car slammed into a rock. Goofy flew into the water. Reaching down, Max scooped him up.

"I'm not your little boy anymore," Max told him. "I have my own life now."

"I know," Goofy answered softly. Max strained to hear above the rushing water. "I just wanted to be a part of it. You're my son, Max. No matter how big you get. You'll always be my son."

Then Max told Goofy everything. About the kids making fun of him. About Roxanne. About the Powerline concert in L.A.

For a moment, the two were quiet. Each one thought about the other one's feelings.

Each one saw things from the other's point of view. They smiled. They understood. They reached out for a hug.

But they missed, for the car was bouncing and spinning all around . . .

They had hit the rapids!

14

The sound of rushing water grew deafening.

"Oh, no!" cried Max. "We're heading for the edge of a waterfall!"

Everything happened quickly. Goofy was flung to shore. But Max! Max was still in the river! Holding tightly to the car roof, Max whirled away.

"Daaaaaad!" he called.

Goofy raced after his son, helplessly. A suitcase flew from the car. A canteen followed. *Clunk!* Something hit Goofy on the head. The fishing rod!

Goofy grabbed onto it. Then he scampered onto an overhanging branch.

"Hurry!" he told himself. "The car is about to go over the falls."

He hauled back and let the fishing line fly.

Just before the car tumbled over, the hook snagged the fender. For a moment, the car hung in the air.

Crack! Goofy's branch snapped in two.

Goofy hurtled into the river. Max and the car plunged down the falls. Max twisted and turned. He held on for dear life. But he wasn't holding on to the car. He was holding their old tent! And now it had wrapped all around him.

Max began to plummet. But the tent billowed out. It lifted Max back up — just like a parachute!

In the rapids below, Goofy held out the fishing rod. "Grab hold, son," he called. "Help me."

Dipping close to the water, Max grasped the rod. Then he landed on the riverbank. Now he just had to pull Goofy in.

Max readied the fishing rod. But the handle twisted off — the part Goofy had been holding!

"Maaaaax!"

"Daaaaad!"

Goofy was swept down the waterfall. A second later, he disappeared into the mist below.

Quickly, Max went into action. It was time for the Perfect Cast.

Ten o'clock. Two o'clock. *Tour jeté*. Twist. I'm a little teapot. The windup. And let her fly.

The hook dropped into the mist. Suddenly, Max felt a tug.

I have something, Max thought. I just hope it's Dad!

Frantically, Max reeled in his catch. Slowly, oh, so slowly, something came into view. Could it be? Was it . . .

Yes! Max pulled Goofy safely to shore.

"Perfect cast!" said Goofy proudly. Father and son — Goof and Goof — hugged tightly at last.

"Boy, this has been a crazy vacation," Max said as the map landed at their feet.

Smiling, Goofy picked it up. "And it's not over yet. We're heading to L.A.!"

15

The next night was the Powerline concert. Roxanne, Stacey, Bobby, and all the kids from school sat in front of Stacey's TV set. "That Goof kid isn't in the audience," one boy said. "Where is he?"

Stacey patted Roxanne on the shoulder. "Don't worry. He'll be there."

Roxanne didn't say a thing. But she crossed her fingers, hoping Max would come through.

In L.A., crowds pressed into the theater.

"Nobody allowed in without a ticket!" a security guard shouted.

Backstage, workers and musicians strode past a pile of instruments. One drum case opened slowly. Max poked his head out. He made sure nobody was looking. Then he scrambled onto the floor. A second later, Goofy jumped out of a guitar case.

"Whew!" said Goofy. "We made it. Now let's get you onstage. I'll go check things out."

"Wait, Dad," Max said. Surely, they'd get caught. Maybe this wasn't a good idea, after all.

"Do you think we should do it, Dad?"

No answer.

"Dad!"

Goofy was nowhere to be seen. But the show was about to begin. Quietly, Max moved closer to the stage. Just one look at Powerline. Then he'd find his dad and go home.

The curtains parted. The stage stood

empty. Suddenly Powerline appeared. Bolts of electricity crackled all around him. The audience screamed.

Powerline opened his mouth to sing.

"Hey, you!"

Max spun around. A guard shined a flashlight in his eyes. "What are you doing back here?"

Max ran.

And Powerline sang.

The stage filled with dancers. The theater rocked, rolled, and hummed with music.

All at once, bolts of electricity crackled next to Powerline. Then Goofy appeared! He had stumbled right into the show!

Goofy looked around, not sure what had happened. He stood there, dazed. Guards were moving in.

"Hey, Dad!" Max hissed from backstage. "Do the Perfect Cast."

Goofy went into the moves. Ten o'clock. Two o'clock. *Tour jeté* . . .

Powerline grinned. "Cool dance!" he said.

Then he copied Goofy move for move. Powerline was doing the Perfect Cast!

Max sighed happily. Goofy would be okay.

Creak! Somebody was behind him. Max whirled around.

"Got you," the guard said, reaching out.

Max grabbed a rope that hung from the ceiling. He swung out over the audience.

"Wow!" somebody shouted, looking at Max. "This concert is great!"

Then Max dropped onstage — right between Goofy and Powerline.

The three nodded to one another. Powerline held up his fingers. "Ah-one, ah-two, ah-three," he said.

And Max, Goofy, and Powerline all did the Perfect Cast. Together. Max laughed out loud. Everything worked out, after all — thanks to his dad.

At Stacey's party, everybody went crazy. Roxanne hugged herself tight. *Max is so great,* she thought. *I can't wait to see him!*

In Pete's camper, P.J. cheered. "He did it! He did it!"

Pete's mouth dropped open. "What do you know," he said. "Maybe there is something to this love thing, after all."

Powerline's song ended with flashing lights and explosions. Smiling at each other, Max and Goofy took a bow.

16

A few days later, Max and Goofy drove back to their hometown. First stop: Roxanne's house.

"Max!" Roxanne cried, running to the door. "I saw you on TV. You were great!"

Max's face lit up. "Yeah? I — "

Then he stopped. He had to tell the truth. "Roxanne, I lied to you. I don't even know Powerline."

"What are you talking about?" said Roxanne. "You were onstage right next to him."

"But I never met him before the concert," Max explained.

"Oh," Roxanne said. "You mean that story about Powerline and your dad. . . . Why would you make that up?"

Max ducked his head. "I wanted you to like me."

Roxanne smiled. "I already liked you."

Max lifted his head.

"From the first time I heard you laugh. Ahyuck!" Roxanne copied the Goof laugh. Then she paused. "So do you want to do something tonight?"

"Definitely!" Max said quickly. But just as quickly, he took it back. "I can't! I'm doing something with my dad. How about tomorrow?"

Roxanne looked over at Goofy. He was checking the car engine. "Deal," said Roxanne. She understood. Max wanted to spend more time with his dad.

Max leaned over for a kiss. "Ahyuck!" he said, after.

Then they heard a shout. Goofy was falling into the car — right on top of the engine. Max and Roxanne rushed over.

Carefully, they helped him out. Goofy grinned, feeling shy. "Ahyuck!" he laughed.

"Your laugh runs in the family," Roxanne told Max.

Max smiled. He was glad it did . . . glad about the vacation . . . glad about Roxanne.

But most of all, Max was glad to be a Goof. Just like his dad.